# ELYON

teddekker.com

# DEKKER FANTASY

## BOOKS OF HISTORY CHRONICLES

### THE LOST BOOKS
*Chosen*
*Infidel*
*Renegade*
*Chaos*
*Lunatic*
*Elyon*

### THE CIRCLE SERIES
*Black*
*Red*
*White*
*Green* (SEPTEMBER 2009)

### THE PARADISE BOOKS
*Showdown*
*Saint*
*Sinner*

*Skin*
*House* (with FRANK PERETTI)

# DEKKER MYSTERY

*Kiss* (WITH ERIN HEALY)
*Blink of an Eye*

### MARTYR'S SONG SERIES
*Heaven's Wager*
*When Heaven Weeps*
*Thunder of Heaven*
*The Martyr's Song*

### THE CALEB BOOKS
*Blessed Child*
*A Man Called Blessed*

# DEKKER THRILLER

*THR3E*
*Obsessed*
*Adam*

# ELYON

## A LOST BOOK

# TED DEKKER
## AND
# KACI HILL

**Thomas Nelson**
*Since 1798*

NASHVILLE   DALLAS   MEXICO CITY   RIO DE JANEIRO   BEIJING

Published in Nashville, Tennessee, by Thomas Nelson. Thomas Nelson is a registered trademark of Thomas Nelson, Inc.

Published in association with Thomas Nelson and Creative Trust, Inc., 5141 Virginia Way, Suite 320, Brentwood, TN 37027.

Thomas Nelson books may be purchased in bulk for educational, business, fund-raising, or sales pro-motional use. For information, please e-mail SpecialMarkets@ThomasNelson.com.

Publisher's Note: This novel is a work of fiction. Names, characters, places, and incidents are either products of the author's imagination or used fictitiously. All characters are fictional, and any similarity to people living or dead is purely coincidental.

Page design by Casey Hooper
Map design by Chris Ward

**Library of Congress Cataloging-in-Publication Data**

Dekker, Ted, 1962-
  Elyon / Ted Dekker and Kaci Hill.
    p. cm. -- (Lost books ; bk. 7)
"A Lost Book."
  Summary: The Chosen Ones need Elyon's grace to face their greatest threat yet, but Darsal is torn between her new mission, trying to love the Horde as Elyon asked her to, and her original one, especially now that Johnis and Silvie no longer seem to be on her side.
  ISBN 978-1-59554-374-5 (hardcover)
  [1. Fantasy. 2. Christian life--Fiction.] I. Hill, Kaci. II. Title.
  PZ7.D3684Ely 2009
  [Fic]--dc22

                            2009007891a

Printed in the United States of America
09 10 11 12 13 QW 6 5 4 3 2 1

# beginnings

O ur story begins in a world totally like our own, yet completely different. What once happened seems to be repeat-
ing itself two thousand years later.

Twenty years have passed since the lush, colored forests were
turned into desert by Teeleh, enemy of Elyon and vilest of all creatures. Evil now rules the land and shows itself as a painful, scaly
disease that covers the flesh of the Horde.

The powerful green waters, once precious to Elyon, vanished
from the earth. Those few who chose to follow the ways of Elyon
bathed once daily in those waters to cleanse their skin of the scabbing disease. For thirteen years, the number of their sworn enemy,
the Horde, grew, and the Forest Guard was severely diminished by
war, forcing Thomas, supreme commander, to lower the army's

recruitment age to sixteen. A thousand young recruits showed themselves worthy and served in the Forest Guard.

From among the thousand, four young fighters—Johnis, Silvie, Billos, and Darsal—were handpicked by Thomas to lead.

Unbeknownst to Thomas, the four heroes were also chosen by the legendary white Roush, guardians of all that is good, for a far greater mission, and were forbidden to tell a soul. Braving terrible battles, crushing defeat, capture, death, and betrayal, they pursued their quest to find the seven original Books of History, a mission that took them from one reality into another.

From their world to the histories, two thousand years into their past, into a city known as Las Vegas, their journey ended deep in the mountains of Romania. On the day after their great victory, having secured all seven books—thereby foiling the plans of the Dark One, who would use the books to destroy humankind—they left our world to return to Thomas and the Forest Guard, two thousand years from now.

But five years have passed since they left their home in the distant future. The world they once knew has changed in favor of their sworn enemy, the Horde. Qurong now rules the city. He has a new high priest—Sucrow, a ruthless servant of Teeleh—to replace Ciphus, who killed Witch. He also has a new general by the name of Marak, sworn to kill every albino on the face of the earth.

Forced to flee the city, Darsal, Johnis, and Silvie have become separated. Worse, Elyon's water, once green, is now red and has apparently lost its healing properties. Johnis and Silvie are soon consumed by the scabbing disease.

To further complicate matters, the Shataiki have mated with some of the Horde, creating a strange race of predatory creatures known as the Leedhan. Insanely jealous of the Leedhan's half-human appearance, Teeleh banished them to the far side of a great river. Outcast and despised, the Leedhan are thought to be gone forever.

But one of them, their embittered queen, named Shaeda, has returned. She has come to seize control of the Horde, and to overthrow Teeleh himself. To do so she needs a human, and she has chosen none other than Johnis as her agent for revenge.

Shaeda seduced Johnis and has fully possessed him. Completely deceived, both Johnis and Silvie have made an alliance with the priest Sucrow with promises of destroying Thomas Hunter and the Circle in three days. But to do so they must acquire a legendary amulet that gives its owner control over the Shataiki.

Meanwhile, Darsal has encountered a different fate. She's discovered the secret of the new red waters—that drowning in its depths heals one of the scabbing disease. Having drowned in the red waters, Darsal has accepted a mission from Elyon: to return to the Horde . . . and love them.

Now our three fallen heroes—Darsal, Johnis, and Silvie—find themselves pitted against each other while the world awaits its fate.

# one

Marak of Southern, Qurong's general over all the Horde army, paced inside one of the bunk rooms reserved for the officers. Two narrow beds stacked on top of each other jutted out of each wall. No windows. Just a torch stand and the candles on his desk. Behind him was a narrow shelf of books.

His captain and best friend, Cassak, was taking too long to bring in the prisoners. He had said he would be here by now. Marak's patience was running out.

"Where is he?" Marak grumbled to himself, storming over to the two open books on the desk. One had once belonged to the long-gone general Martyn, who'd trained him; and the other, to his dead betrothed, Rona.

How, in Teeleh's name, had everything gone wrong in a week? He was a general, for goodness' sake, respected and trusted and feared. He'd been a good man with a loyal brother and a soon-to-be wife.

And now . . .

General Marak had sequestered himself in the officers' hall at the north end of Middle, with fifty warriors standing guard. For two days they had roasted in the hot sun, choosing loyalty to their general over the orders of the Dark Priest. And for two days all of Middle remained tense, caught in the battle lines drawn between High Priest Sucrow and Marak.

Marak took a long swig of his drink and continued his trek around the room. The meal his slave had brought him earlier sat untouched on the table. He couldn't eat; his stomach felt as if it were full of knives.

He went to the door and swung it open. "Is Darsal here yet?"

"No, sir," the warrior replied, falling into his salute. "We've not yet seen—"

"Find her."

"My lord—"

"Find her!" Marak shut the door and went back to his inner tirade. This was a mistake. All of it. He'd had everything under control a week ago. At least, as much as the mess left by his predecessor allowed.

In less than a week, the priest had undone everything Marak had built, all in a bizarre sense of revenge and power play. Marak hadn't wanted to defy Qurong—and technically he hadn't. He had no reason to. But a series of events had led him to defy the

Dark Priest and sequester himself in the officers' quarters. Now Qurong, the supreme commander, must hear him out on the absurd notion of a general taking orders from a priest. He had to.

Knotting his fist and glowering at the cold plate of food, he reviewed this plunge into dishonor.

First, upon gaining rank over Marak, Sucrow had ordered him to execute his own family—all albinos. Marak had stalled as long as possible, but Sucrow was powermongering.

Marak's jaw tensed at that thought. It'd been some time since he'd given the order and stood by as Cassak administered the hideous potion—Marak's albino-killing concoction called the Desecration—to his family. His brother.

He whirled around to the door and thrust his head out again. "Why are you still standing there?" he barked at the guard. "Did you find her?"

"The albino is still out on your previous orders, General," the guard replied cautiously. "I've sent a scout for her."

"Good." Again Marak turned back to his predicament. Where was he . . . ? Oh, right. His second problem. Sucrow had struck a deal with this Josef character from the backside of the desert, who claimed to have a better, faster way of killing off the albinos: a magic amulet made of Leedhan magic—whatever that was—that would give control over the mythical Shataiki and command them to wipe out the blight that is the albinos.

Marak had dismissed the idea. Sucrow had not.

Which led him to his third problem: Sucrow had taken Josef

and Arya and had gone after the amulet without him. Immediately upon learning this, Marak sent his captain, Cassak, after them. If Sucrow was so convinced and so willing to risk his life for this amulet, there had to be some merit to its power.

Acting upon Marak's order, Cassak had captured Josef and Arya and taken the amulet from them. The move had infuriated Sucrow, so Marak had moved into the officers' quarters, barred the windows, and set guards around the sundial for his and his prisoners' protection.

So here he was. For two days Sucrow had made no move, but that would not last.

So be it. Marak had the amulet and the two prisoners, Josef and Arya, in his custody. His slave, Darsal, knew them as Johnis of Middle and Silvie of Southern, but he did not. Whatever their reasons were, he would not yet let them know he had that information. A knock at the door snapped him out of his silent rant.

"Who is it?" he growled.

"Darsal. Let me in."

Darsal, his albino slave, had been in the cells the same night his family was executed and had spoken with them before their deaths. She wore his brother's Circle pendant around her neck, his gift to her. Marak wasn't sure why he'd spared her, but he had. Twice. Once that night, when she vowed to be his slave. The second time in a glen, shortly after Sucrow had ordered him to kill her and, to his horror, he found he could not.

This at least partly explained his rationale to sequester himself here in the officers' quarters. Qurong might not yet know Darsal was still alive despite Sucrow's orders. And Sucrow couldn't use her in his sadistic rites—or worse yet, kill her—if Marak still had her.

"Marak, are you going to let me in?" The knob was rattling. He quickly crossed the room to unhook the latch and swing the door open.

There she was. This albino slave, this woman . . . Darsal of the Far Northern Forest, who claimed to have crossed time and space through worn leather portals called the Books of History. She stood before him, arms crossed. Morst covered her exposed skin, and a blue veil wrapped around her head, covering her nose and mouth. Rich brown eyes watched him, noticeably frustrated.

"Thank you," she said. "You summoned me?" Their eyes met.

If he wasn't mistaken, he was falling in love with her. With an albino. This was most definitely a mistake.

He forgot what he'd summoned her for. He released a breath and worked the knot of frustration and anxiety back down into his belly.

"General." Darsal spoke softly, pulling him out of his thoughts. The citrus scent she wore drifted through the room.

Oh. Right. He was a general with a thousand problems to take care of. Unwilling to be caught in her warm gaze again, Marak stormed down the dark hall to the war room.

"Has Cassak arrived yet?" he asked her as he shoved the door open, not missing a step.

"Not yet," Darsal said, straightening the blue veil. She watched his irritated pacing, characteristic of the last several hours. He circled around the eight-foot oval table made of cherrywood. A green runner draped the width of the table, laid squarely beneath three copper candelabra. White pillars of wax flickered as curls of smoke drifted through the war room.

"He'll be here," Darsal said.

He tugged at the collar of his rust-colored tunic, sweaty and itchy, and turned toward the east-facing window he'd had Cassak's men bar and cover with a heavy crimson drape so no one could see in. Every window in the building had received the same treatment. The room was dark, but he couldn't very well light the torches without suffocating them all. Why Darsal would unnecessarily coat herself in morst, then drape a veil over her head in here, was beyond him.

Her fruity scent mingled with that of the candles.

"Relax, Marak. He'll be here."

*Focus.*

"He's certainly taking his time about it. Read the message again," he ordered, turning back to her.

"It hasn't changed, my *general.*" Darsal quirked a brow, completely exasperated with him. Her veil slipped, revealing dark brown braids. "He'll be here with your amulet and your prisoners."

"Just read it. I don't have the patience for your obstinacy. Not today. Not when we're at the brink of a civil war and Sucrow is halfway to Qurong by now. If your so-called friends hadn't been so stupid—"

"It was the Throaters' fault, and you know it. Cassak said so himself."

"They were only out there because they're a bunch of superstitious religious idiots who convinced the priest one of his own myths might be true," he argued.

"Jordan believed Shataiki exist," Darsal pushed. Marak tensed. "And the Roush. And Elyon. Was your brother a fool, Marak?"

Marak scowled at her. "Jordan was mistaken on many things. That didn't make him a fool."

"Yet you call drowning foolish."

"Your persistence is aggravating."

She studied him. "You're missing the point of all of this, my general."

"What's that?" He almost regretted the question. He knew her answer.

"This is about—"

"Elyon. You keep saying that."

"More than that, Marak. I mean, yes. But you're still missing it. Elyon doesn't just love the Circle. He loves the Horde too. You. This is all about you and Elyon. That's why I'm here." She opened her arms wide, indicating the room. "All of this."

Marak started to protest but was interrupted by a knock at the door. Secretly he appreciated the diversion from her nonsense about being Elyon's emissary. "We don't have time for this. Who is it?" he growled, unwilling to open the door on a whim.

"A messenger from the captain, General!" a familiar voice called through the door. Cassak's favored scout.

Marak nodded at Darsal, who let the scout in. She'd taken to staying by the door, even so far as to sleep in front of the threshold at night. A curious thing.

The small warrior saluted and went to one knee. Marak bid him stand, then bellowed, "He's late."

"He was avoiding the Throaters," the scout explained. "He's bringing the prisoners from the southeast to avoid further confrontation with the rebels."

Marak queried him on Eram, the half-breed rebel, then came to his real question. "When will Cassak be here?"

"Shortly, sir. He's making sure the prisoners and the amulet are secure. He's already sent messages to the commanders so they can respond to the rebels accordingly."

"Tell me something," he asked the scout. "Were you there?"

"Yes, sir."

"Exactly what did you see?"

"Well, sir, it was just like the captain's report said."

"And no one would obey the captain?"

"Oh, *we* did, sir. We didn't kill any of them. Warryn and his men did the killing."

Marak bit back a comment. "What else? Cassak kept talking about black trees and clouds."

The scout didn't answer. He kept looking at Darsal. Staring. What was this scout looking at Darsal for?